For those I love
T. C.

Pour Robin
M. F.

Text copyright © 1997 T.C. Bartlett

Illustrations copyright © 1997 Monique Felix

Designed by Rita Marshall

ISBN 0-89812-522-7

This new edition published in 2004 by Creative Paperbacks

123 South Broad Street, Mankato, MN 56001 USA

Creative Paperbacks is an imprint of The Creative Company.

Printed in Italy.

The Library of Congress has cataloged the earlier edition as follows:

Library of Congress Cataloging-in-Publication Data

Bartlett, T.C.

Tuba lessons / by T.C. Bartlett ; illustrated by Monique Felix.

"Creative Editions."

Summary: While walking through the woods on his way to his tuba lesson,

a boy becomes sidetracked by all the animals that want to hear him play.

ISBN 0-15-201643-0

[1. Animals—Fiction. 2. Tuba—Fiction. 3. Stories without words.]

I. Felix, Monique, ill. II. Title.

PZ7.B28433Tu 1997

[E]—dc21   96-44584

First Paperback Edition

5 4 3 2 1

TUBA

T.C. BARTLETT   illustrated by MONIQUE FELIX

LESSONS

CREATIVE PAPERBACKS

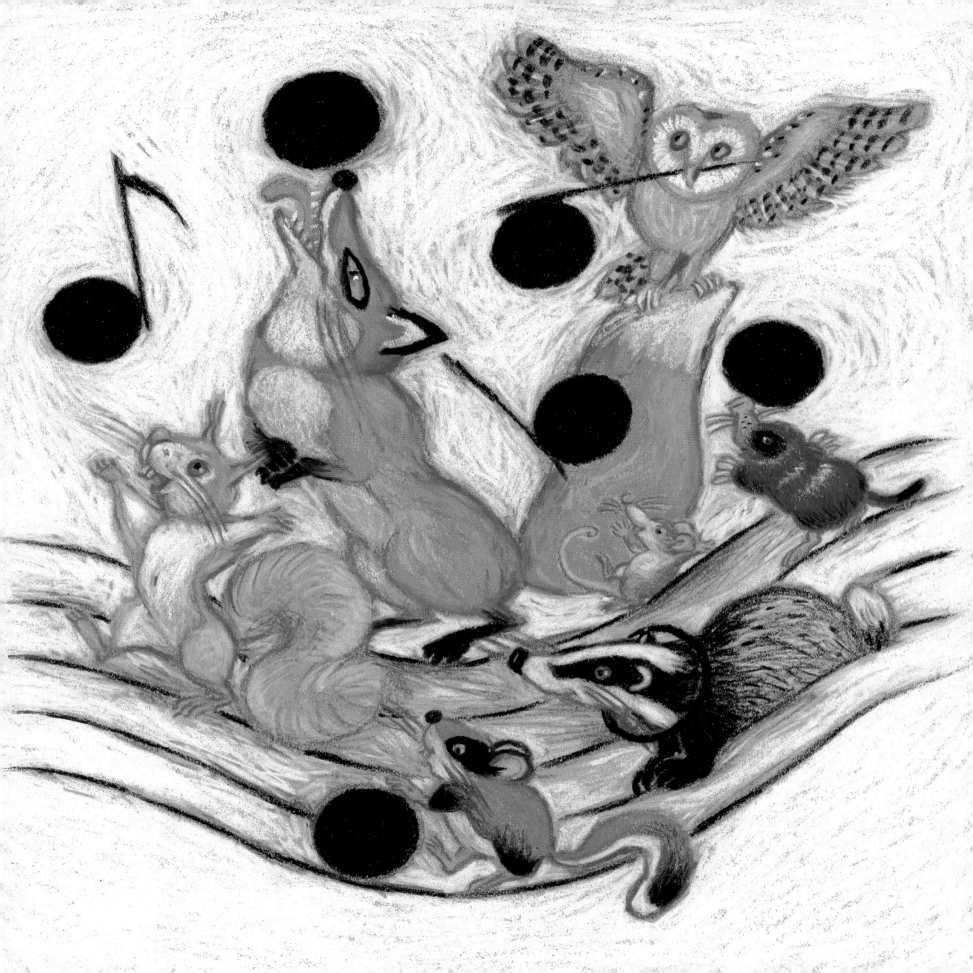

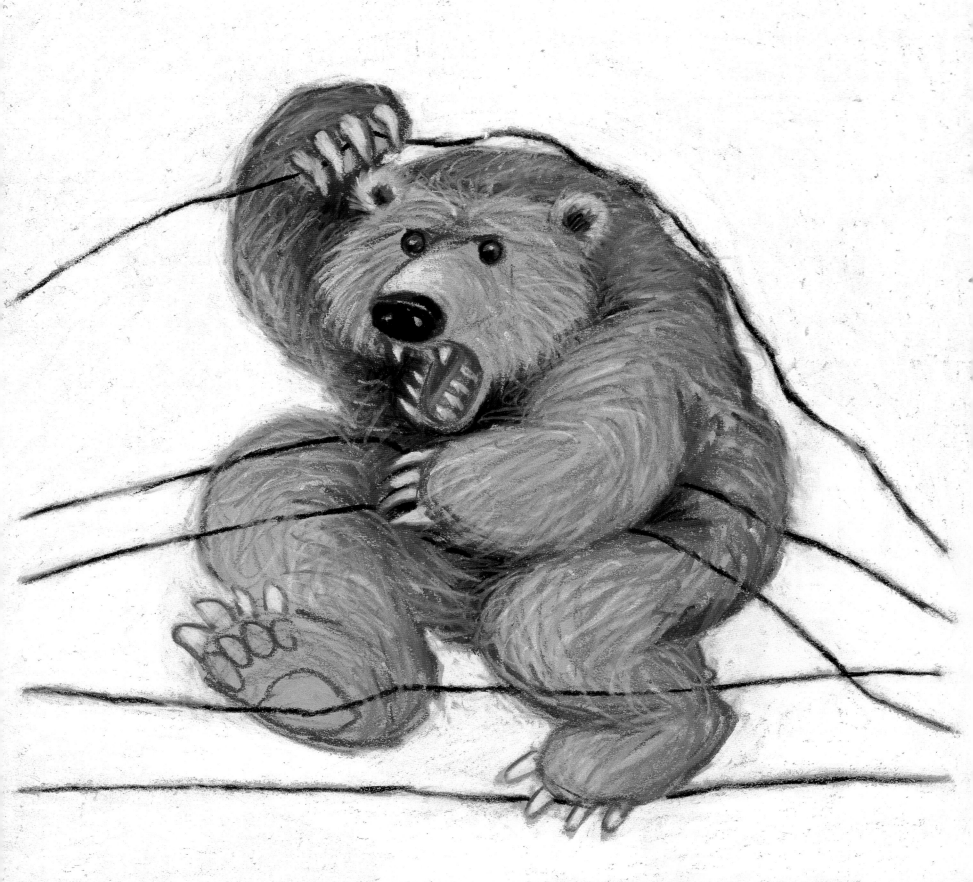

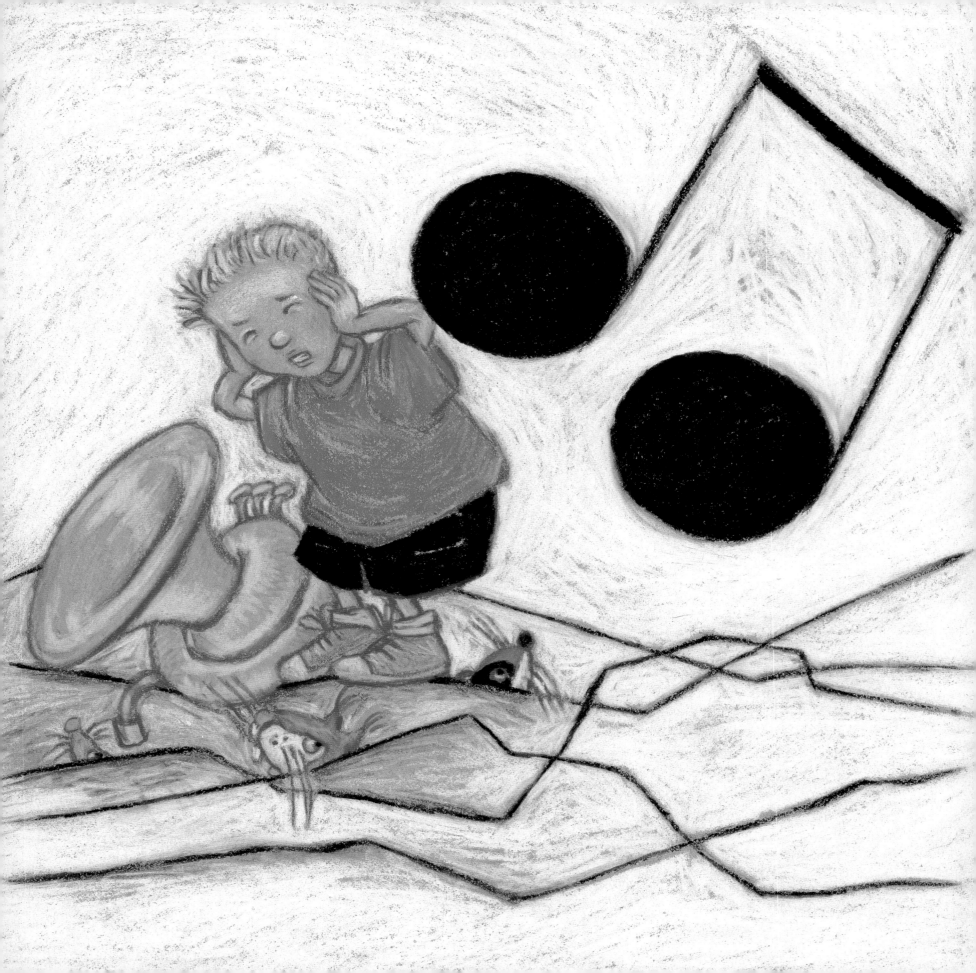